1/12

ATHENEUM BOOKS FOR YOUNG READERS
An imprint of Simon & Schuster Children's Publishing Division
1230 Avenue of the Americas, New York, New York 10020

Originally published in Great Britain by Oxford University Press

The text for this book is set in Vag Rounded and Family Dog.
The illustrations for this book are rendered digitally.
Manufactured in China
0511 OUP
First U.S. Edition 2012
10 9 8 7 6 5 4 3 2 1
CIP data for this book is available from the Library of Congress.
ISBN 978-1-4424-3614-5

I don't want to be a pea!

This is a story of **Hugo** and **Bella**

written by
Ann Bonwill
illustrated by
Simon Rickerty

Atheneum Books for Young Readers • New York London Toronto Sydney

**All hippos have birds,
and Bella is mine.**

Correction.

All birds have hippos,
and Hugo is mine.

Anyway. Where was I? Oh yes, tonight is a very special night.

It is the night of the Hippo-Bird Fairy-Tale Fancy Dress Party.

You mean the
Bird-Hippo
Fairy-Tale Fancy
Dress Party.

Whatever.

The important part is we have decided on a costume.

We are going to go dressed as the **Princess** and the **Pea**.

Don't we look lovely?

But I don't want to be a pea.

It is too green and small.

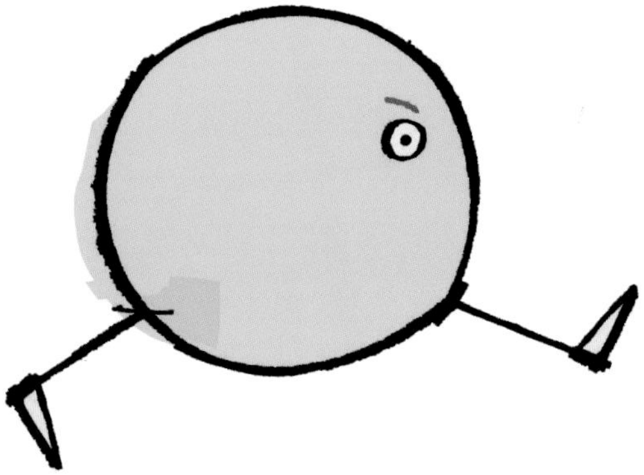

Instead I will be a . . .

mermaid and you will
be my rock.

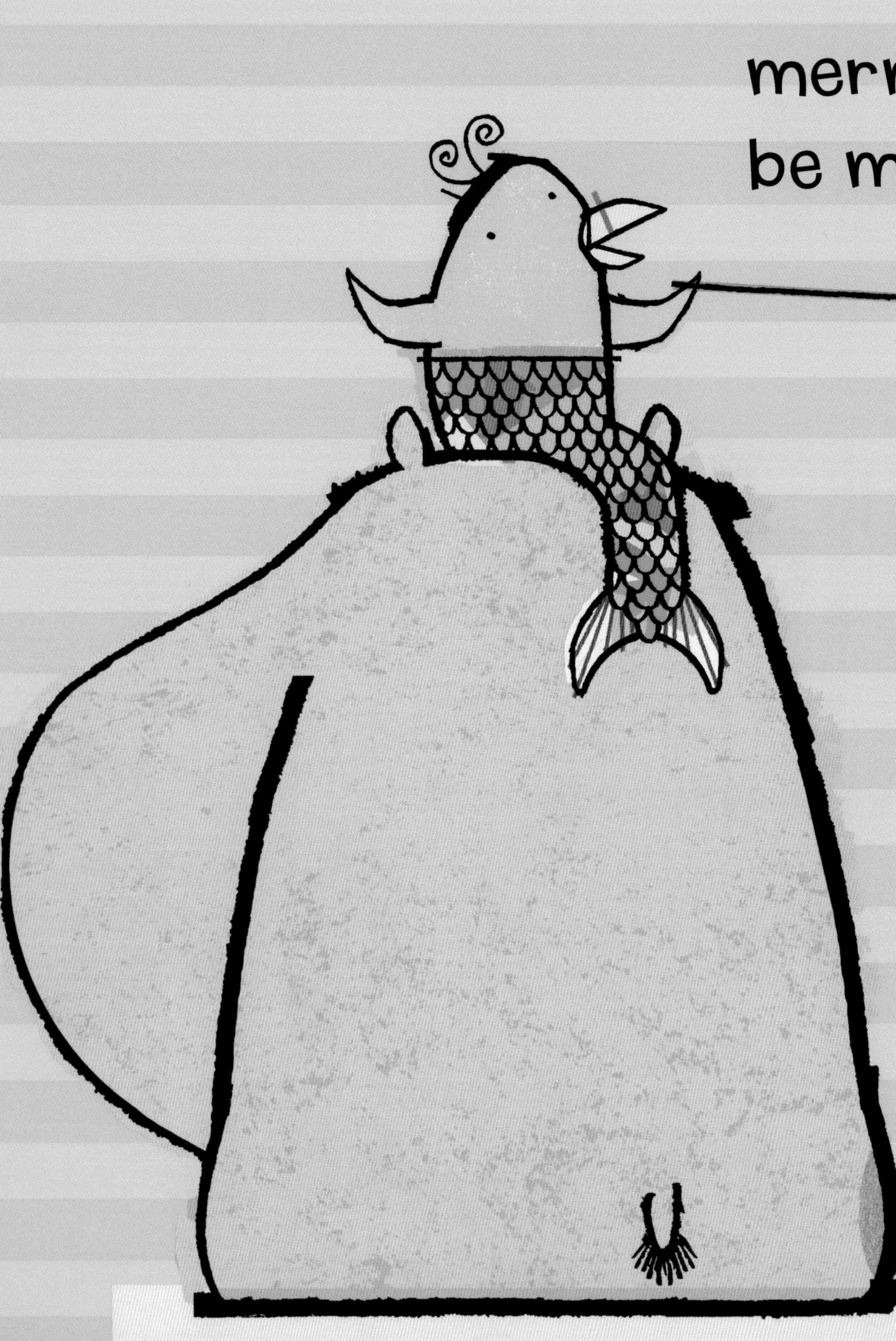

You make a
very fine rock.

**I don't want to
be a rock. It is too
gray and blobby.**

But you are gray and blobby.
I will ignore that comment.

How about a king and his jester?
You look smashing!

I
look
ri-**dic**-ulous.

We are **NOT** going to be a king

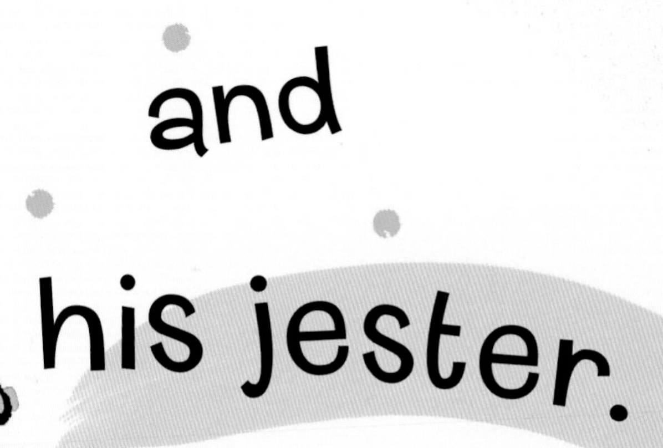

and

his jester.

Let's try . . .

Cinderella
and her pumpkin.

**I will not
be a pumpkin.
Look how very
orange I am.**

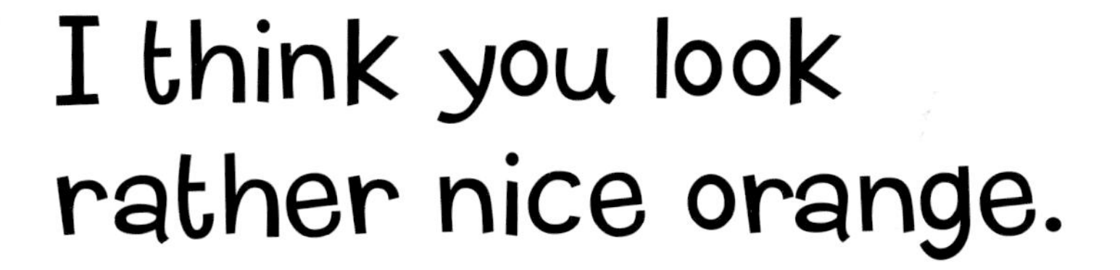

I think you look
rather nice orange.

Thank you.
But I will still
not be a pumpkin.

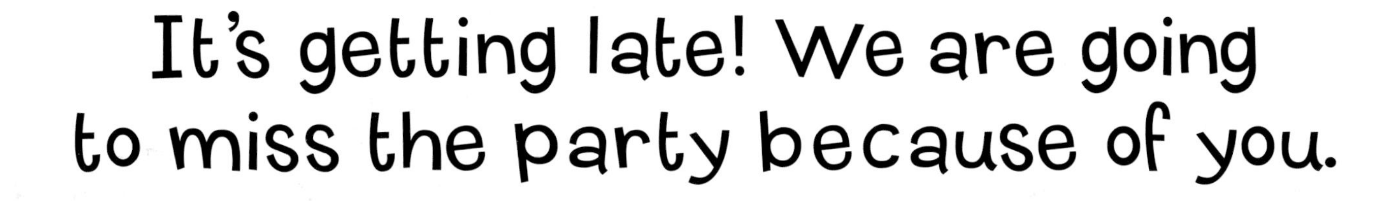

It's getting late! We are going
to miss the party because of you.

If we miss the party,
it will be because of you.
You are the one who refused
to be a **pea** in the first place.

If you like peas so much,
then you can be the **pea**
and I will be the **princess**.

Besides, I don't even
want to go to the party
with you anymore.

Well then, neither do I.

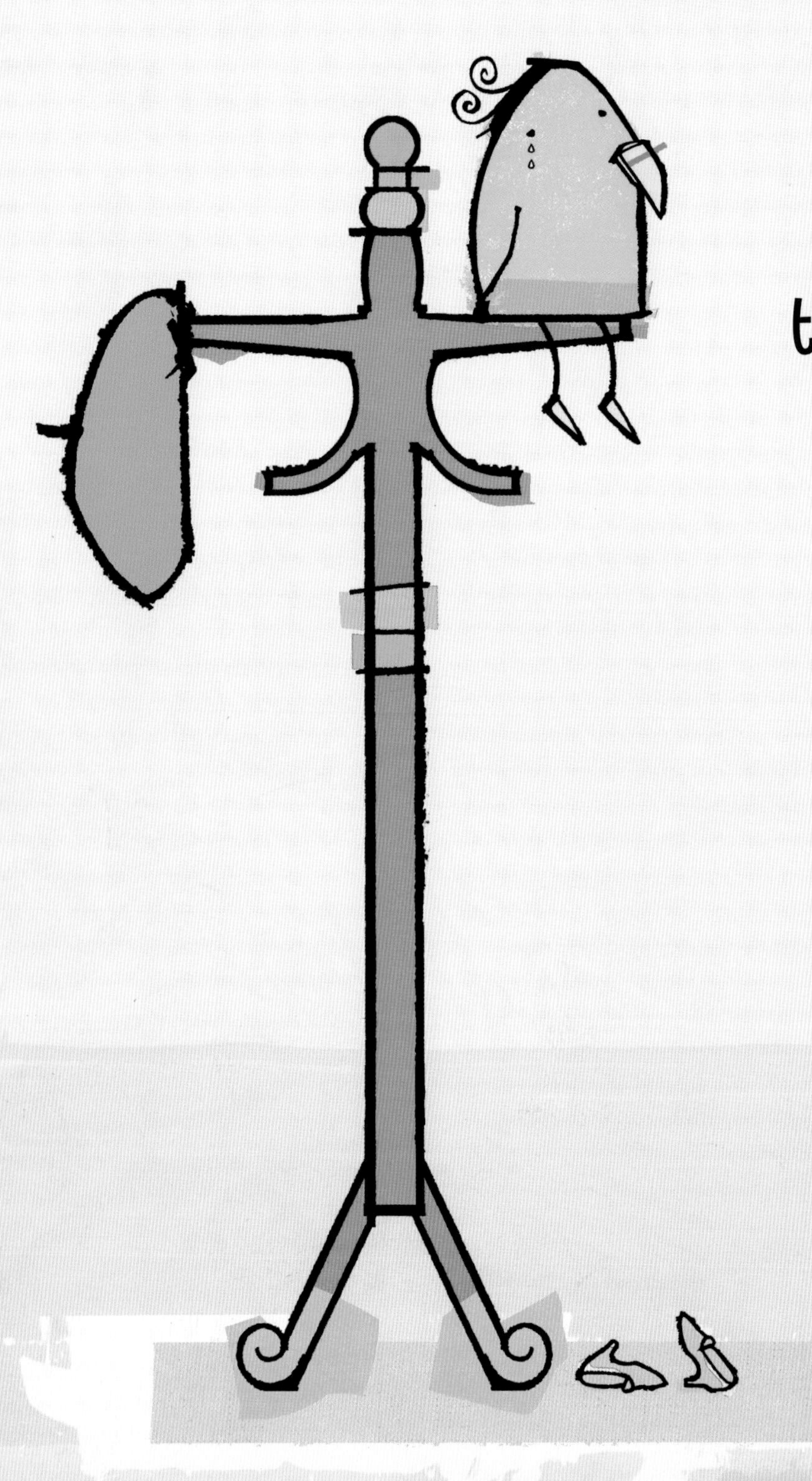

I've never been to
the Bird-Hippo party
without Hugo.

Perhaps I could be a **pea** after all?

The party won't be
the same without Bella.

And she would make a
beautiful **princess**.

What a strange costume!
Who are you? asks
Big Bad Hippo.

AND who
aRe YOU?
asks
LittLe Red
RidiNg BiRd.

I am Hugo,
Bella's hippo.
I am Bella,
Hugo's bird.

And we've come to the fancy dress party as . . .

the happy ending!